READ ALL OF THE
BLONDIE MCGHEE MYSTERIES

BLONDIE McGHEE

#4
Pressure to Perform

Ashley Eneriz

CONTENTS

Prologue

In case you missed the end of Blondie McGhee 3: Growing Suspicion...

"Can you believe it," I say, turning to my sister. "Lizzy Lizard is within a mile of us. I have never been so close to a superstar before!"

"Just wait until you see where your seats are, then you will really be excited" my dad chimes in.

Jana and I look at each other, both trying hard not to squeal in excitement.

Dad was right. Jana and I squealed when he showed us our seats. "VIP seats for my two very important people," Dad laughs.

I knew dad worked at the Epic Center, but his job is in accidental management. I always thought his job was boring, and even the days I visited him in the office, it seemed like all he did was sit at his desk. I had no idea that he got to actually see celebrities.

"This is the best day ever," I squeal, giving my dad a tight hug.

"And after the concert, we get to go backstage and meet Ms. Lizard," my dad adds.

"What?" Jana screams. She can no longer pretend she is too cool to be here. She is just as excited as me.

"Do you think she will let me have her autograph?" I ask.

"I bet she will," my dad answers.

We sit down in our seats and watch the opening act. It was a boy band from Britain that I had never heard of. All of the girls in the crowd screamed but not me. I was saving my voice for Lizzy Lizard.

After the boy band exited the stage, the whole arena went pitch black and two bright spotlight shone on the stage.

"Here she comes," I exclaim as I hold on tightly to my dad's arm.

"Alright, who's ready to party?" Lizzy Lizard's voice came booming out of all the speakers. The crowd went wild. I could see her blonde, curly hair and sequin outfit as she started walking towards the front of the stage.

"Then let's put our hands…" Lizzy's voice cuts off as she falls to the floor with a loud thud. Screams echo through the audience and a lot of confused voices fill the air. The band members race over towards her.

"Stay here!" dad yells as he pulls out a walkie-talkie that was hidden in his jacket.

"Team, we have an emergency situation. Lizzy is down. Security standby and get ready to escort all individuals out. Accident management team, we need all hands on deck, call emergency services and keep the crowd calm. I'm going to make an announcement," my dad shouts into his walkie-talkie.

He makes his way on stage and bends down to talk with the band members who are huddled over Lizzy. He then takes the microphone and faces the crowd.

My dad has always said he has stage fright, so it was a complete shock when he spoke so confidently in front of the thousands of people in the Epic Center.

"Attention, please. We are sorry to inform you that the concert will be postponed tonight. Lizzy Lizard is ill and has fainted, but she will be all right. We are going to get her to the hospital now. On behalf of the Epic Center, we apologize for this inconvenience. You will be contacted in the next few business days in regards to rescheduling your show or receiving a full refund."

The Epic Center starts filling up with people shouting questions and other words I could not make out. My dad puts his hand out towards the crowd.

"I know you are all worried and upset by the events tonight, but in order for us to do our job and get Lizzy the care she needs, we need you to leave in an orderly fashion. Security guards will help guide you to the doors. All bathrooms except the one in the main lobby have been closed, and we will be guiding you out through the main lobby. Thank you for your cooperation."

Just then the lights on the stage went black while the lights on the audience brighten. I see someone with bright pink hair duck behind the stage.

"Did you see that," I ask Jana.

Jana's mouth is wide open, and her eyes are glued to the spot where the pink-haired lady disappeared.

"That's Myra," she says hoarsely. "She was just standing in front of us."

"Which means I don't think Lizzy Lizard's accident was an accident after all," I say.

CHAPTER ONE

Rock Star Down

Well, my dream has finally come true. But instead of being within arms distance of my all-time favorite singer, Lizzy Lizard, I am standing next to the spot she passed out twenty minutes before. So much for a concert.

Since my dad is in charge of safety, he has kicked into high gear. I've never seen him in action before. I just thought he did a lot of paperwork for a living.

"Alright, all Epic Center staff and volunteers, you are expected to stay until the police have taken your statement. If you are missing when it's your turn for questioning, consider yourself on the top of the suspect list and looking for a new job for due diligence. "

This is what happens when my dad watches too many

shows about cops and lawyers. He starts using "suspect" and "due diligence" in the same sentence.

"Dad, is everything going to be all right?" I ask when he breaks away from the other Epic Center employees.

My dad runs his hand through his hair and exhales deeply.

"Don't worry, kiddo. It will all be fine. I'll call your mom to come and get you. "

"No, please don't. I can help you." I beg.

"Sweetheart, that is very sweet, and normally, I would love your pro detective skills, but tonight there is a lot at stake. I need to get this mess settled and find the cause behind this before the press run the story tomorrow."

"Dad, are they going to fire you?" Jana, my older sister, asks.

"What? No, that's not fair. It's not your fault!" I scream.

"Calm down, calm down," my dad says in a hushed voice waving his hands downward.

"But you said they fired the guy before you because he made a big mistake," Jana adds.

My dad sighs heavily.

"Girls, please don't worry about that..." My dad starts to

say but is quickly interrupted by a woman wearing a headset and three different walkie-talkies on her waistband.

He puts a finger up to show he will be right with her and then turns to us.

"Take my cell phone and call your mom to get you. Also, tell her that if she needs to get a hold of me, call me on my work cell. Though please let her know that things are a bit in crisis mode right now, so only call if it's crucial. Okay?"

Jana and I nod, and Jana takes the phone out of my dad's hand.

"And no texting your friends, Jana," my dad warns quickly.

"Okay, okay," Jana replies but my dad is already in a conversation with the headset lady. They are both talking quickly with a lot of hand movements.

Jana throws herself in a nearby seat and scrolls through my dad's cell phone. "Where did all those games go?" she asks, not looking up.

Without waiting for an answer, Jana sits up and says, "I guess I should just call mom. "

"No!" I blurt out. A few Epic workers glance over but then quickly go back to what they were doing.

"It's just if you call mom then she will pick us up and we will have to go to bed."

"And?" My sister asks, looking slightly annoyed.

"Don't you want to help dad?"

"Um, I guess, but there isn't much we can do," she answers.

"That's what you think. I packed my emergency detective kit," I say showing her my backpack.

"What? I thought you told dad you packed snacks for the concert," Jana points out.

"Well, I did, but my main purpose was to make sure my detective kit was packed."

Jana nods with a smirk on her face.

"Well, it's a good thing I did. Now we can solve the case and save dad's job," I say, still trying to convince her not to call mom.

"And what if we get in trouble?" Jana asks, still unsure.

"I'll take all the blame. I'll tell mom and dad that I forced you to do it," I say.

Jana doesn't say anything.

"Please, please, please," I beg.

I am about to drop to my knees for dramatic measure, but before I do, Jana holds up her hands.

"Okay, okay," she says. "But we better not run into dad."

"That will be easy," I exclaim. "I installed a tracking app on both of dad's phones when he kept losing them last month. All you have to do is open it up, put in the password, and then you can see where dad is."

"What's the password," Jana asks.

"Blondieis#1, of course," I say. So far Jana was proving to have fewer detective skills than Emma, my dachshund sidekick.

"Okay, if we are going to work together, I need you to follow a few detective rules," I explain.

"Oh brother," Jana says, rolling her eyes.

"I'm serious, Jana. This is really important stuff."

"Fine, but I am not talking in an accent, wearing a hat, or saying anything silly, like you do," she answers.

"I don't do any of those things," I lie. I feel my cheeks

heat up slightly. *Had Jana been spying on me when I pretended to solve cases in my room?*

I clear my throat, "Detective rule number one, do not touch the evidence. Your fingerprints will prevent the real culprit from being caught."

"Have you ever caught someone off of their fingerprints?"

"Well, no, but one day I will. Like I was saying," I continue, slightly annoyed. "Detective rule number two, document everything. Little details are not meaningless. They could be the key to solving a case."

"Where am I supposed to write stuff down?"

"Lucky for you, I brought an extra pen and notebook," I say, excitedly opening up my bag. *Maybe Jana was getting into the whole detective act after all.*

"Lucky me," Jana says with a bored tone. *Or maybe not.*

"Finally, the most important detective lesson of all," I say as I hand her a notebook with glittery owl on the cover. "Make sure you have all of the facts before you make an accusation. Got it?"

"Yep, where do we start? I really want mom to pick us

up before that ice cream store closes."

Mmm…double fudge sundaes do sound perfect right now. No, focus. Lizzy Lizard.

"Since dad went that way," I say pointing. "Let's start on the stage."

Jana climbs on the stage and looks closely at the floor.

"What exactly are we looking for?"

"Clues!" I exclaim.

"How will I know when I find a clue?" she asks.

"You'll just know."

"Here's a wrapped piece of gum," she says picking it up from the ground.

"Jana!" I exclaim.

"What? What did I do?"

"First of all, you touched the evidence with your fingers. You should have picked it up with your pen and notebook or asked me for one of my gloves."

"Sorry," she laments.

"And secondly, that's just trash. Everyone chews gum." I say.

"Okay, sorry," she says and stuffs the gum wrapper in her pocket. *Eww, was she really going to eat that later? Older sisters can be so gross sometimes.*

I slowly scan the stage floor to see if I can see any other clues. A drop of water falls on my head.

"What in the world?" I say out loud, placing my hand on my hair and looking upward.

"What's wrong," Jana asks.

"I felt something wet drop on my head, and I think it came from that orange bucket in the rafters."

Jana looks up and immediately and shields her eyes. "How can you see anything up there? The lights are too bright?"

"Try looking past the lights," I tell her.

Jana closes her eyes. "The lights really hurt my eyes. Besides, it was probably nothing," she says, walking off the stage. "The stage doesn't have any good clues, Blondie."

"Don't give up yet, please," I beg.

"Who said anything about giving up?" she grins. "I was just going to suggest we search Lizzy Lizard's dressing room."

"Jana, that's a brilliant idea!" I exclaim. "You really are getting into this detective stuff."

Jana flashed a sly grin. "I just really want to see what her dressing room looks like."

"Me too," I say, trying not to squeal with excitement.

CHAPTER TWO

Frenemies

"I can't believe we are going inside Lizzy's actual dressing room," I say, twisting the door knob slowly. This is the closest I have ever been to a celebrity. The fact that it is my all-time favorite singer is even cooler.

I catch a glimpse of pink hair as soon as I open the door. "What are you doing in here?" I gasp.

Right there on the couch with bright pink hair, lizard print boots, and an ombre blue and green dress was pop star Myra.

As soon as Jana saw who I was talking to, she gasped too.

All of the magazines Jana reads say how much Myra and Lizzy hate each other. In fact, just last week one of Jana's magazines reported that Myra was trying to get back at Lizzy for stealing her song.

Myra looks up at us sadly. Her deep purple eyeliner and glitter eyeshadow were smudged and her face looked puffy.

"Are you alright?" I ask, taking a step towards Myra.

"Blondie, she probably hurt Lizzy," Jana whispered, trying to grab my arm.

Jana had a good point. "Did you hurt Lizzy?" I ask, stepping back again. I've never confronted a real criminal before. Who knows how dangerous she could be.

"No!" Myra shouted. "Lizzy is my best friend."

"That is definitely a lie," I say. "Everyone knows you guys hate each other's guts."

"Yeah and here is just one magazine cover to prove it," Jana says picking up a copy of Teen Music off the table. The cover has a picture of Lizzy and Myra's face with a graphic lightning bolt between the two of them. The headline reads, "Only One Can Make It in Hollywood."

Myra throws her head back and laughs loudly. "All magazines are fake news," she explains.

Jana and I look at each other and then back at Myra. I cross my arms for extra emphasis, showing Myra that I'm not buying her story.

"Lizzy and I are frenemies," she says.

"What?" Jana and I ask at the same time.

"It means that we are best friends in private and pretend like we are enemies in front of everyone else."

"But why would you want to do that?"

"It makes us more popular," she says flipping her pink hair back.

"I'm still confused," I say.

Myra laughs again and grabs the copy of Teen Music out of Jana's hand. "Do you think these trashy magazines..."

"Hey, they aren't trashy," Jana interrupts, grabbing the magazine back quickly.

"I'm sorry," Myra says, holding up her hands defensively. "I didn't mean to offend you. I just meant magazines don't want to publish stories about best friends. They want to publish stories about celebrities fighting and doing embarrassing things. That's what sells copies."

"But doesn't that hurt your image?" I ask.

"Surprisingly no!" Myra exclaims. "The more we are in magazines, the more people love us. Sometimes we will even crash each other's concerts because it drives up sales to the next concert."

"Is that why you are here tonight?" I ask. "Were you crashing Lizzy's concert?"

"No! I promise!" Myra says. "I just came to keep Lizzy company afterwards. And then she…" Myra grabs a tissue off the side table and dabs her eyes.

"Do you know of anyone that would want to hurt Lizzy?" I ask.

"Gosh, no. Everyone loves her."

"No crazy fans or disgruntled employees?" I ask. I

picked that word up from a detective show I watched last weekend with Grams, my mystery-loving grandma that got me my first detective kit.

"There are always crazy fans, but nothing out of the ordinary that I can think of," she says.

"So, you can't think of anything weird or out of the ordinary that happened today?"

"Now that you mention it," Myra says, shifting on the couch. "Lizzy did yell at the wardrobe assistant before her concert."

"What did she say?"

"Something about how she would be lucky if anyone hired her after today."

"But why did she say that?" I ask.

Myra shrugs her shoulders and grabs a bottle of water from the table. "Beats me," she says as she unscrews the cap. "It was close to the time her show was about to start, so I just went to her dressing room to get out of the way."

"Do you know where we can find this wardrobe

assistant?" I ask.

"Try looking in the room marked wardrobe down the hall, and let me know if you find out anything."

CHAPTER THREE

Missing Shoes

"I wonder where dad is," Jana asks.

My eyes grow wide. I completely forgot about him. I quickly touch the cell phone's screen a few times and breathe a sigh of relief. "He's in his office, on the other side of the Epic Center."

"Now we just need to find the wardrobe assistant and hear her story," I say.

Jana groans.

"Come on, Jana. You heard Myra. It sounded like Lizzy was going to fire her, which means she was probably mad enough to hurt Lizzy."

"I'm just tired of running around, Blondie. Do you really think you are going to find out who tried to hurt Lizzy? Maybe it was just a freak accident."

How can she even think this way?

"Well, I am going to see what I can find out from the wardrobe assistant before jumping to any conclusions," I say, trying not to feel angry towards Jana. "Can you at least wait here and watch the phone to make sure dad doesn't come this way?"

"I guess," Jana says, slumping down on the floor. She quickly glances at the phone and then puts it beside her so she can read the issue of *Teen Music* she swiped from Lizzy's dressing room.

I don't have time to worry about Jana and her sudden bad mood. I have to make sure the wardrobe assistant didn't get revenge on Lizzy.

I walk quickly down the hall, looking at each door, but none of the doors say anything about wardrobe.

"Ouch!" someone yells as I bump into them. I was too busy looking at the doors to see a young woman with glasses carrying a large pile of clothes.

"I'm so sorry. Are you okay?" I ask.

The girl looks surprised. "Yes, I'm fine. Thanks for caring." She smiles and starts to walk away.

"Wait," I call out. "Do you know where the wardrobe room is?"

"Why?" she asks.

"I'm looking for Lizzy Lizard's wardrobe assistant."

"That would be me. Or at least, it's me until I am officially fired. Why are you looking for me?"

"I just wanted to ask you a few questions about what

happened today."

The wardrobe assistant looks me up and down. "And you are?" she asks sarcastically.

"My dad works here, and I am just trying to help him find out what happened so he doesn't lose his job," I blurt out. I hadn't meant to share so much.

"Come with me," she says dryly.

I follow her a few doors down. "Open that door, will ya?"

I open the unmarked door. "Is this the wardrobe closet?" I ask.

"Yep," she says, pushing her arm full of clothing inside.

"Why isn't it marked?"

"Well, after what happened, I was told to take everything down and pack everything away. I was told that there would be no more shows this week."

"Who told you that?"

"Lena sent me a note. She's Mr. Maguire's assistant. I'm Kim, by the way."

"Blondie," I reply. "Do you happen to have that note?"

Kim throws the clothes down in an opened, oversized trunk, and pulls out the note from her pocket and hands it to me. "I'm not sure why I should even bother packing, since I don't think I have a job anymore."

"What happened?" I ask, grabbing the note. I am tempted to pull out my notebook, but I don't want her to stop talking.

She sighs and throws herself on one of the leather sofas. "Just the same old, annoying stuff," she says, taking off her glasses and rubbing the bridge of her nose. The way she talks reminds me of Jana, and without her glasses, she doesn't look much older than Jana does.

"You can tell me. I'm a great listener," I encourage her.

She shrugs. "I can't see what damage it will do telling a seven-year-old my problems."

"Nine and a half," I correct her.

"Same difference," she laughs.

Before I can tell her that there is a big difference between seven and nine and a half, she sits up and starts to talk. "This was my dream job," she says. "I was going to be working with my favorite singer, doing what I loved, putting together amazing outfits."

"Only, it really isn't much of a dream come true," she continues. "All I do is steam clothes, clean shoes and accessories, and make sure everything is ready for the real stylist. No one even notices me unless something goes wrong."

"Did something go wrong tonight?" I ask.

"Oh yes!" she says. "The stylist was sick today, which meant I was in charge of everything. Everything was going smoothly until right before the show."

"What happened?" I ask.

"All of Lizzy's shoes disappeared except one pair. She always wears her signature lizard boots to start her show, but they were gone. The only shoes that were there were her metal, spiked heels. She was so mad and said that I stole them all."

"And did you?" I ask, cautiously.

"Of course not! Lizzie wears a size six, and I wear a size nine. There is no way her shoes would fit me."

"Can you think of anyone who would want to take Lizzy's shoes?"

She shakes her head. "I know her outfits look glamorous from the audience's point of view, but all of her stage shoes are pretty worn out, especially her lizard skin boots."

A light bulb went off in my head.

"Lizard print boots?" I say excitedly.

"Yes, the ones she always wears for the opening of her concerts. She says they bring her good luck or something like that."

"The green and bronze ones that go up to the knee?"

"Those are the ones. Why?"

"I think I might know who took them. Thank you so much for your help."

CHAPTER FOUR

Locked In

I run out the door before the wardrobe assistant can say anything else, shoving the note she gave me in my pocket. I don't have time to give it back to her. I have to find Jana.

I spot her sitting where I left her, almost finished with her magazine.

"Jana," I yell, startling her.

"What is it?" she asks, holding her hand to her chest. "Why are you yelling?"

"Because you were wrong," I say slightly out of breath.

"About what?"

"What happened to Lizzy was not an accident." I tell her about the missing shoes and how she wasn't wearing her famous lizard print boots.

"What does that have to do with anything?" she asks.

"She wasn't wearing her lizard print boots," I say again.

"I heard you the first time. I'm not deaf," she retorts.

"Do you remember who was wearing those boots?" I ask.

"Myra," we both say together.

"We have to go back to her dressing room to find her," Jana says, picking up the magazine and cell phone.

As soon as we reach Lizzy's dressing room, we hear a man's voice inside.

"Wait, where does the phone say dad is?" I ask, pulling her away from the door.

Jana inhales sharply. "Oops," she whispers.

"You haven't been checking?" I accuse her.

"I'm sorry. I was too busy reading the story about Lizzy and Myra. You'll never believe…"

"Jana, we don't have time to for silly magazine stories. Check the phone."

She quickly opens up the app and gasps.

"It shows dad's dot being on top of our dot," she whispers.

"He's probably in there," I whisper. "We have to hide."

"Please open," I say as I grab the door knob across from Lizzy's dressing room. The room was a small electrical closet with hardly enough room for both Jana and I.

"The door won't close all the way," Jana says trying to squeeze in.

"It's okay. Just be as quiet as possible. Maybe no one will notice."

After a few minutes, we hear muffled voices and footsteps.

"Don't breathe," I say.

"I thought I told Robert to lock all of the electrical closets before the concert," a voice that sounded like my dad says.

I can't see much in the cramped, dark closet, but I know Jana's eyes are bulging at me as she grabs my wrist. I squeeze myself as far back into the closet as possible, gently pulling Jana towards me. We feel the door push against us, and I turn my feet and face sideways so that the door will close.

"Remind me to tell Robert to fix this closet after this fiasco has died down," the voice says.

"Sure thing, John," a woman's voice replies.

We wait another minute before we let out a big exhale.

"That was close," I say. "Now let's get out of here before we suffocate."

Jana reaches for the door knob and tries to turn it, but the door doesn't open.

"Oh no, it won't open," she says panicking. "We are stuck in here forever."

"Calm down, Jana," I say.

"How can I calm down? I feel like I am being squished to death."

"Just listen to me. We will get out of here. First, feel the door knob. What does it feel like?"

"Like a door knob. I don't know," Jana says anxiously.

"I mean, can you feel any grooves or holes or locks?"

"I think I can feel a small line."

"That's great news. That means that the door can be easily unlocked from the inside. It must be a safety feature. Try sticking your nail in the line and twisting."

"But I just painted my nails," she whines.

"Jana, focus."

I hear her scrape her nail along the door knob but do not hear the door unlock. "Ouch!" she yells.

"What happened?"

"I tore my nail off."

"Can you try a different nail?"

"Blondie, it hurts so bad. Why don't you do it?"

Stay calm. I tell myself trying to remember not to get mad at Jana. This detective stuff is all new to her, so I shouldn't expect too much from her.

"I'm going to try and lean over you and unlock it, okay." I can't see Jana's face clearly, but I can tell she is nodding. I stretch my arm as close as I can to the door knob, but it's no use, I can't reach.

"I can't reach it," I say.

"What are we going to do?" Jana cries.

"I have an idea. Let me see your magazine."

"Now you want to read the magazine."

"Of course not. I'm going to break us free." I say. Jana hands me the magazine, and I jab the sharp edge towards the door knob.

"Come on," I tell the magazine, trying to get the edge in the lock line. Jana starts to breath heavily, and I can tell she is starting to really panic now.

"Why don't you tell me about what you read in the magazine," I say, trying to calm her down.

Immediately her breathing regulates and she excitedly tells me what she read. "The magazine said that Myra and Lizzy's agent was tired of them fighting and was only going to represent Lizzy."

"Do you think that's true? Myra said those magazines were lies," I say, trying to unlock the door.

"Well, she could be the one lying," Jana accuses. "Plus, it would make sense. Their agent, Rosh Maguire, is one of the best. Last year, he dropped the band, Real Boyz, and they ended up breaking up."

"Hmm," I say, trying to piece together the clues while also trying to figure out the annoying lock.

"Think about it. If Maguire drops Myra, then she could end up with no career. But, if Lizzy is out of the way, then Maguire would have to keep Myra, meaning she would stay successful."

Finally, I am able to turn the magazine in the lock completely and a satisfying click sound fills the air. Jana grabs the door knob and pushed the door open, gasping dramatically for air.

"We did it," Jana says.

"You mean, I did it." I correct her.

"Look at this! I tried my best," Jana says angrily. She holds up her finger for me to see her damaged nail. Half the nail is gone, and the area is bloody and red.

"Jana, I'm so sorry," I say, feeling bad for thinking she was just being baby.

"Let's just go find Myra. I want to get this over with and go home," she says.

CHAPTER FIVE

The Secret Announcement

"Myra?" I call into Lizzy's dressing room. Myra was

still on the couch, making funny faces at her phone.

"Oh hey, girls," she says happily. "Just uploading some

pictures for my fans. Find anything exciting?"

"Do you want to tell us about your boots?" I ask.

"Oh, these things. Not really my style, but whatever."

"Why did you take them from Lizzy?"

"Take them from Lizzy? What do you mean? She gave them to me."

"When?"

"They were waiting for me when I got in her dressing room."

"How do you know they were for you?"

"Because she left a note. See," she grabbed a crumpled note off the table and handed it to me.

The note read, "Myra, you should totally wear my lizard boots tonight for when you come on stage. Love, Liz."

"I thought you said you weren't going to sabotage her concert tonight," I say.

"I wasn't."

"Then why did she say you were going to go on stage."

"Because we were going to make an announcement at the end."

"Announcement? What announcement?" I ask.

"It was supposed to be a secret until we announced it," she says. She takes a big sip of water and places the bottle back on the table. I make a mental note to grab the bottle for evidence, just in case the police need it later.

"We know that your agent was going to drop you," I say, hoping to catch her in her lie.

"Drop me? Are you crazy?" she laughs. "I make that man a lot of money."

"It says it all on this magazine cover," I say.

"How many times do I have to tell you that those magazines are full of lies?" she says, looking angry.

"It can't all be lies," I say, not sure what to say next. "The magazine can't just pull this stuff out of thin air."

"You're right," she says. I wait for her to continue, but she just drinks more water.

"What do you mean?" I prod.

"Our agent tells the magazine the stories."

"But why would he do that?"

"To make more money, of course," Myra laughs.

"I can understand the other stories, but why would he tell the magazine that he was going to drop you?"

"I was wondering the same thing. I thought the story might have been true, so that's why I brought it to show Lizzy after the show. I wasn't sure if maybe Lizzy had changed her mind about the..." she stops talking and looks at her phone.

"The what?" Jana asks.

"I can't tell you," she says.

"If you don't tell us, then we just have to tell the police that you have motive for hurting Lizzy," I say, hoping it will encourage her to talk more.

"Fine. I'll tell you," she sighs. "Lizzy and I were going to start our own label and ditch our agent. Then I read *Teen Music* this morning, and thought maybe Rosh had caught on to our plan and offered Lizzy more money. But then, I got her note and boots and knew we were still on for our announcement."

I looked at the note in my hand again.

"I just don't understand why Lizzy would send you this note and still be so mad at the wardrobe assistant for losing her boots. It just doesn't make sense. Are you sure she wrote you this note?"

"Who else would write it?" Myra asks.

"Does it look like her writing?"

"I don't know. I guess."

"Look at it again, does anything look weird to you?" I ask, trying to remain patient.

"I guess it was weird that she called herself Liz. She hates that nickname. I just figured she was in a hurry."

I need to find a writing sample of Lizzy's to compare it with the note. I walk over to her dressing room table and start opening up the drawers.

"What are you doing? You can't just go through her stuff," Myra says.

"I'm trying to find a sample of Lizzy's writing," I explain.

"Why?" she asks. Myra might be a great singer, but she is definitely not a good detective.

I remember the other note from my pocket and pull it out. "Everyone writes differently, even if it looks the same. Some people curve or angle their letters one way, while another person might not dot their lowercase I's. Take these two notes for example," I say, smoothing both pieces of paper on the table in front of Myra.

"They look exactly the same to me," Myra says.

"That's because you aren't looking hard enough," I say, slightly annoyed. "Look how the L in Liz…" I stop talking. Myra was right. The handwriting in the notes were identical. Both notes even had the same use of "Liz."

"Blondie, what is it?" Jana asks, looking over my shoulder.

"The notes are written by the same person."

"That's what I just said," Myra laughs.

"But why would Lena forge a note to Myra?" Jana asks.

"We need to find Lena and ask her," I say.

"That should be easy. She posts on social media about a hundred times a day," Myra says, picking up her phone. She quietly taps on her screen and then says, "There. Found her." Myra bursts out laughing.

"What's so funny?" I ask.

"Lena's wrote, 'One day we'll be the famous one.'"

Myra laughs some more, showing me the picture. "That girl sings like a snoring whale."

I look closer at the picture. Lena is smiling with her arm over Kim."

"That's the wardrobe assistant," I say. "Come on, Jana, let's go see if they are in the wardrobe closet."

I dash down the hall trying to remember which unmarked door that Kim took me through. "I think it's this one," I say, hoping I am right.

It was hard to tell if I was in the right room because there were no clothes or accessories scattered around like earlier. "Can I help you?" a voice calls.

I turn around and see the wardrobe assistant.

"Kim. I was looking for you."

"Yep, I'm still here," she laughs. "Thankfully I am finally done packing everything up."

"Everything except that purple feather outfit," Jana points out.

"Oh, that thing," she laughs. "It reeks of cigarette smoke. Yuck! I don't know who's that is. Lizzy hates purple and definitely doesn't smoke." Jana keeps looking at the outfit, but I ignore her. I am focused on finding Lena.

"Anyways, I was wondering if you just took a picture with Lena," I ask.

"Oh yeah, I did. How did you know?"

"That doesn't matter. Do you know where she is now?"

"I think she said something about getting a smoothie at the concession stand for Mr. Maguire."

"Thanks," I call out, not answering her question. I grab Jana's arm and pull her outside the door.

"We need to find Lena before she gets too far away," I say. "Do a dad check, will you?"

Jana pulls out the phone quickly and taps the screen while I lead the way. "We are clear. Dad is not close to us."

"Perfect. Now it's time to figure out why Lena would steal Lizzy's boots and send that fake note."

CHAPTER SIX

Gross Gum

"I think that's her," I say, pointing to a red-haired girl that looks like the picture Myra showed us.

"Excuse me," I say sweetly. "Are you Lena?"

"I am. How can I help you?"

"I just had a few questions, if you have a minute."

"Make it quick. It's been a crazy night."

"Do you recognize this note?" I ask, showing her the crumpled note written for Myra.

"Nope," she smiles. "It looks like Lizzy wrote it to Myra."

"Nice try. I know you wrote it because the handwriting matches the one you wrote to the wardrobe assistant."

Lena shakes her head. "Hmm…I guess it does look familiar. I only just write what Mr. Maguire tells me to write. I am his assistant after all."

"Why would Mr. Maguire want you to steal Lizzy's boots and forge a note to Myra?" I ask.

Lena shrugs. "Mr. Maguire just told me he was trying to patch up their relationship before the concert. He said he was sick of seeing them fight and ruin each other's careers."

"But Myra and Lizzy are really friends, aren't they?"

Lena laughs. "Haven't you ever read an issue of *Teen Music*? Anyways, I've got to run. Da…I mean, Mr. Maguire will be needing my help."

"It sounded like she was about to call him Dan," Jana says after Lena is out of sight.

"You're right, but Mr. Maguire's first name is Rosh. Something doesn't seem right." I say. "Let's try to follow her."

"I don't know about this, Blondie. Plus, I'm starving," Jana says, shoving her hand in her pocket and pulling out the piece of gum from earlier.

"You aren't really going to eat that, are you?" I ask.

"Not unless you want to have it," she laughs, shoving near my mouth.

"Gross," I say, pushing her hand away. "Come on. We are going to lose Lena." I dart down the hall I saw Lena go down. I can hear Jana walking loudly behind me.

Lena is about twenty feet in front of us when she stops in front of a door. She looks around her and then pulls out a key card.

"Yuck, gross!" Jana shouts.

"Jana," I say in a hushed tone. "Shhhh!" Thankfully, Lena went into the room and didn't hear Jana's outburst.

I turn and glare at her. "Are you trying to get us caught?"

"I'm sorry," she says, holding her hand out. "This gum was so disgusting and it started burning my tongue."

"That's why you don't eat mysterious stage gum," I say.

"Something is seriously wrong with this gum," Jana goes on.

I sigh and hold out my hand. "Do you still have the wrapper?"

Jana digs in her pocket. "It was just a plain white wrapper," she says, handing over the crumpled-up wrapper.

I smooth out the wrapper and hold it up to the light. "There's something written on it," I say.

"Now Quit," I read, squinting to see the words.

"What kind of gum brand is that?" Jana asks.

"Isn't that the gum Uncle Peter chewed when he was trying to stop smoking cigarettes?" I ask.

"You're right!" Jana exclaimed. "Good thing it worked for Uncle Peter because that was the most disgusting thing I have ever tried in my life."

"Now that we have your gum mystery solved, we need to get back to the real mystery," I say. "We need to see what Lena is doing behind that door."

"How are we going to get in? She used a key card," Jana asks.

"Watch and learn," I grin.

"Wait, Blondie," she calls out.

"Come on. It will be fine."

As I approach the door, I see that the door has "Rosh Maguire – Local Agent" scrawled in gold letters.

"I didn't know Mr. Maguire actually worked here," Jana whispers.

"Maybe that's why he's so afraid of Lizzy and Myra becoming their own label. There aren't any other local singers around here."

I inhale sharply and bang on the door.

"What are you doing?" Jana whispers panicking.

"Shhh," I say, holding my finger to my lips. "Trust me."

The door swings open, and Lena frowns when she sees me.

"Oh, it's you again. I didn't know you worked over here," I say innocently. "I am just trying to find the bathroom."

"There was a big one near the smoothie concession stand you were just at," she says, looking slightly annoyed.

"It's out of order," I blurt. "Don't you have a bathroom in your office? Please? I really have to go."

"Fine, but be quick," she says, opening the door wider. She points to a small bathroom in the office, but I try to look at everything before going into the bathroom. Nothing unusual stands out.

I sulk into the bathroom. This case is starting to look like a dead end. *Wait a second!* I instantly think when I see an orange bucket in the bathroom. *That looks like the same bucket that dropped water on my head from the stage.*

I flush the toilet to make Lena believe I am using the bathroom and not collecting clues. As soon as I turn on the sink faucet to pretend wash my hands, something in the trash can catches my eye. It is a torn-up photo of Lizzy and Myra.

"It's getting late. You should probably find your parents and leave," Lena says as I exit the bathroom.

"My sister has to go to the bathroom too. If you don't mind."

"No, I don't..." I nudge Jana before she can finish her sentence.

"I mean, I don't want to be a burden, but I don't think I can hold it any longer," Jana says running into the bathroom.

"Kids," Lena says, shaking her head. Before she can say anything else, her cell phone rings.

"Yes," she snaps. "No, I told you to be here at 11:30 tonight to take Mr. Maguire to the airport. He changed his flight to the red eye an hour ago. Don't be late," she commands as she hangs up the phone.

"Mr. Maguire is going to Brazil tonight even though Lizzy is in the hospital?" I ask.

"That is none of your business," she says.

I notice a pack of Now Quit gum sitting on a package of cigarettes. "Is that your desk?" I ask, trying to sound nonchalant.

"No, of course not. I'm just the assistant. That's Mr. Maguire's desk."

I reach out to grab a picture frame on the desk and feel a big shock. "Ouch," I say, shaking my hand.

"That's why you shouldn't touch…" Before Lena can finish her sentence, Jana comes out of the bathroom.

Lena never finishes her thought but instead says, "Thank goodness. You really need to go now." She gently places a hand behind my back and lead me towards the door.

"Thank you so much," I manage to say before she closes the door in our faces.

"Jana, I think I finally know who tried to hurt Lizzy, but we need to get back to the stage."

CHAPTER SEVEN

Clue Review

"Blondie, slow down. What if dad catches us?" Jana says trying to keep up with me as I run towards the stage area.

"If he does, then I can tell him what really happened."

"Well, are you going to at least tell me what really happened? I am kind of in the dark over here," Jana says breathlessly.

"As soon as I check something on the stage. Keep up!"

The stage was further than I had thought, and my feet were feeling tired from running. I didn't even know what time it was or where my dad was, but I knew I was so close to solving what had happened.

I place my hands on my knees as soon as I get on stage. Good thing I haven't been slacking in P.E. class or else I might have passed out before I even got to the stage. I can hear Jana panting behind me.

"What did you have to check?" she asks.

I point up. "The orange bucket, is it still there?" I take a few deep breaths before looking up myself.

"What orange bucket? I don't see anything."

I walk over to the place where the water dropped on my head and look up. The bucket is not there anymore.

"The orange bucket is gone," I say quietly. "Which proves my theory right."

"Blondie, you aren't making any sense," Jana says, sounding frustrated.

I pull out my detective notebook and pen from my backpack. We spent so much time running around this past hour, I didn't have a chance to write anything down. I broke my own detective rule.

"Let's start with the things we know," I say, jotting down my thoughts. "We know that Lizzy fell and had to get medical help. We know that Myra and her are planning on breaking ties with their agent, which makes him the top suspect."

"But you don't have enough proof that Mr. Maguire did it. You are just going off of what Myra said."

"That's where you're wrong," I explain. "The orange bucket that dropped water on my head earlier looked exactly like the orange bucket in Mr. Maguire's bathroom. Mr. Maguire also had a whole package of Now Quit gum on his desk - the same gum you found near where Lizzy fell. Plus, I heard his assistant talking on the phone saying about Mr. Maguire going to Brazil tonight."

Jana gasps. "It must have been him. Why else would he flee the country right after a concert."

"Exactly," I nod.

"But how did he hurt Lizzy? Last time I checked, dropping water on someone's head isn't life threatening."

"Remember the metal shoes?"

Jana gasps again.

"I am guessing Mr. Maguire wanted the whole thing to look like an accident, so he electrocuted her with a little bit of water, a loose wire, and her metal shoes. Everyone else would be safe, but Lizzy would be like Benjamin Franklin flying his kite in a thunderstorm. She attracted the electric shock because of her shoes. I bet the loose wire is over there," I point.

"Jana, Blondie, what are you doing here?" an angry voice calls. All the hairs on the back of my neck stand up.

"Oh no, it's dad," Jana whispers.

CHAPTER EIGHT

Wrongful Accusations

"Dad!" I say excitedly. "You're never going..."

"What are you two still doing here?" my dad commands, cutting me off. My dad is not alone. He is standing with three other men in suits, his walkie-talkie clutched tightly in his hand.

"Don't be mad," I say, waving my hands in front of me. "I know you told us to call mom, but we found out who hurt Lizzy."

"I told you not to worry about Lizzy and to go home, and you didn't obey," he continues. I notice there are several deep creases in his forehead. I don't think I've ever seen him this mad before.

"Please, will you just listen?" I beg.

"You have five minutes to explain what you found."

"Lizzy's agent, Mr. Maguire, hurt Lizzy to get back at her for starting a label with Myra." I blurt.

"What?" one of the men standing next to my dad shouts. "I did not do any such thing." At that moment, I realize that I had never seen a picture of Mr. Maguire and didn't know what he looked like. If I had known he was standing right next to my dad, I would have asked to talk to my dad in private.

"Blondie, Mr. Maguire was on a private jet when Lizzy fell," my dad explains.

"He did it," I say. "There was a piece of Now Quit gum on the stage and a package of the same gum on his desk."

"Now Quit? Isn't that for smoking? I don't even smoke." Mr. Maguire says.

"Well, then how do you explain how I saw an orange bucket dripping water on the stage and now the bucket is in your office's bathroom?"

"How did you get into my personal bathroom?" he asks, looking shocked.

"That doesn't matter. Just tell the truth, Mr. Maguire. You didn't want to lose Lizzy and Myra, so you electrocuted Lizzy to scare her a little bit." My cheeks are on fire, and I realize I am jabbing my finger in the air at Mr. Maguire.

"John, you need to control your daughter," he says, looking at my dad.

"I'm so sorry, Rosh. I'll take care of it. Blondie, like I said, Mr. Maguire wasn't anywhere near the Epic Center when Lizzy fell. He just got here twenty minutes ago. I think you owe him an apology," my dad says, looking at me intensely.

"But, but," I stutter.

"I know who really did it!" Jana shouts from the other side of the stage. I had been so busy accusing Mr. Maguire that I didn't see Jana leave my side.

"It was Lena," Jana continues, holding up a purple feather.

"Lena?" My dad, Mr. Maguire, and I all say at the same time. *Oh no, what is she doing?*

"Yes. You see," she starts, imitating my detective voice. "When Blondie and I talked to Lena earlier, I thought she was going to call Mr. Maguire Dan, but I just realized she was going to call him dad."

"Huh?" I say.

"Lena is your daughter, isn't she Mr. Maguire?"

"Well, yes, but.." Mr. Maguire says, sticking his hands in his pockets nervously.

"And is she trying to quit smoking?" she asks.

"She told me she quit five months ago to improve her vocals," he says.

"And does she happen to own a purple feather outfit?" Jana asks.

"Yes, but what does this have to do with anything," Mr. Maguire stammers.

"Please, Mr. Maguire," I beg. "We need to know."

"Yes, she has a purple feather outfit. She performed two songs for the opening act tonight. Didn't you see her?" he asks.

"No, the opening act was that boy band from Britain," my dad says quietly.

"What?" Mr. Maguire shouts. "Who allowed them on stage?"

"Lizzy did," a girl's voice said behind him. Lena steps in front of us and glares at me. I can hear her smacking her gum, and when I am brave enough to sneak a look at her, I notice a stray purple feather tucked in her hair. *How did I miss that earlier?*

A horrified look runs across Mr. Maguire's face. "Oh no, Lena. You didn't…you couldn't have…did you? Mr. Maguire struggles to get out the words.

"Oh dad, I didn't mean to send Lizzy to the hospital. I just wanted to give her a little shock and ruin her first set."

"And then you tried to frame Myra for doing it, didn't you?" I ask, remembering the lizard boots and note.

"She deserved it," Lena replies.

Mr. Maguire put his head in his hands and rubs his eyes. "No, no, no," he says hoarsely.

"I would have gotten away with it all too, if it wasn't for you nosey kids. In two hours, I would have been happily on my flight to Brazil."

"Security, please send two officers to the stage area please," my dad talks into his walkie-talkie. He then turns to one of the men on his left and says, "Please inform authorities that we have the suspect who hurt Lizzy."

"But, it was just an accident," Lena calls.

"I'm sorry," my dad says. "This was no accident. You knew what you were doing."

"But it's not my fault," Lena yells. "She's the one that canceled my one chance to perform." When no one said anything, Lena continued. "Dad, come on. Her and Myra were going to fire you. You were going to lose your job. Why won't you take my side?"

Mr. Maguire shakes his head and looks down at his pointed leather shoes.

Jana and I watch in silence as two large security guards approach the group.

"Please handcuff Lena Maguire and take her into holding until the police arrive," my dad says.

"Dad," Lena pleads. "Please, do something." Tears start rolling down Lena's cheeks. "It was an accident," she says hoarsely.

"I'm sorry, Rosh," my dad says, putting his hand on Mr. Maguire's shoulder. "I had no idea."

Mr. Maguire just nods and walks after the security guards and Lena.

"Jana, you solved the case," I shout, grabbing her into big hug. It takes Jana several seconds to hug me back. She's not exactly a touchy-feely kind of person. "We did it together," she says.

"As for you two," my dad says, clearing his throat. "What am I going to do with you?"

"Dad, I'm so sorry," I say. "We just wanted to help."

"Jana, I thought you knew better," my dad says sternly.

"I..uh…" Jana stutters.

"No, it's not her fault," I say. "I made her do it."

My dad turns to the other men. "I'll be back in an hour. Please get in contact with Lizzy's family to find out how Lizzy is doing and to explain what happened. Also, please have PR draft up a few statements for me to look over when I get back." The men nod and walk away from my dad.

"As for you two, let's go," my dad says grumpily.

CHAPTER NINE

Facing the Consequences

"How long are we going to be in trouble?" I ask my dad once we are in the car. Jana kicks my ankle. "Ouch," I whisper, rubbing the spot she kicked.

My dad lets out a big sigh. "Well, I have to talk with your mother first, but I would expect being grounded for a month."

"But we were just trying to save your job, Dad," I whine.

"I know, Blondie, and I appreciate it. As much as I hate to admit it, you both saved me from a huge headache back there."

"So, does that mean we aren't in trouble?" Jana asks hopefully.

My dad laughs. "Oh no, you are still in trouble, but maybe the punishment can start tomorrow. For right now, let's find an ice cream shop before everything closes."

"Did you learn anything from tonight?" my dad asks before shoveling a huge bite of ice cream in his mouth.

"Yes!" I shout. "Rock stars are a lot of drama."
"I'm never going to smoke because then I might have to eat that disgusting gum again," Jana says.

We all laugh and take another bite of ice cream.

"I'm serious," my dad says. "While I'm thankful for your help, you both went behind my back and disobeyed me. It's going to take some time for me to trust you both again."

"We know, dad, and we are really sorry," Jana says, looking down into her ice cream.

"Do you think there will be another Lizzy Lizard concert?" I ask.

"For you two? Definitely not. For the rest of the city, well, things are a bit of a mess right now, especially if Lizzy really is leaving her agent."

"Solving the case was fun," I say. "But I would have much rather seen Lizzy perform."

"Me too," says Jana.

CHAPTER TEN

One Last Mystery

My parents grounded Jana and I for a month. Do I think it's fair? I'm not sure how I feel about it.

On one hand, I did disobey, but on the other hand, I did solve an amazing case. I guess that's the life of a true detective, you have to take the good with the bad.

"Knock, knock," my dad says, slowly pushing my door open.

"Hey, sweetheart. Get ready and get in the car," he says with a mischievous smile on his face.

"Where are we going?" I ask.

"You'll see," he says. "You don't have to solve every mystery, you know." He chuckles as he walks away. I can hear him knock on Jana's door down the hall.

I know my dad says that I don't have to solve every mystery, but I just can't help it. It is as if my brain is made to process clues and try to figure out the puzzle as quickly as I can.

He can't possibly be taking us to another Lizzy Lizard concert, since it has only been two days from the accident. I really don't think he will be rewarding us with more ice cream either. Not that I would mind another sundae right now, but isn't the whole point of being grounded to be locked in your room?

"Jana, do you know where we are going?" I whisper, as I buckle my seatbelt. She ignores me and looks out the window. I can tell she is still a little bitter about me getting her grounded, but I'm not sorry. It was the best time I ever had with my sister.

The car ride is unusually awkward since no one talks, and I am afraid to ask all of the questions that keep popping into my head.

After what feels like an eternity in the car, we pull up to the largest house I have ever seen. I look over to Jana to see if she will look at me, but she is too focused on the large house. Her eyes look wide, and I think I even heard her gasp.

My dad pulls up to a security booth and shows a man his ID. The man nods and pushes a button that opens up the gate.

We drive up a long drive way, past a stone fountain of two dolphins, and in front of a porch that is bigger than my room and Jana's combined.

A small, curly blonde woman waves frantically at us from the porch.

"Is that..." Jana starts asking with wide eyes.

"Lizzy Lizard!" I shout, answering her question with my own surprise reaction.

"No way," Jana says.

"Yes, way," my dad says. "She wanted to meet you after she found out what you did."

"Hi, there," Lizzy calls as we get out of the car. "I am so happy to meet your girls, John."

"Nice to…uh…meet you, Miss Lizard," Jana says nervously, sticking her hand out for a handshake.

Lizzy laughs loudly and grabs Jana in a hug. "Don't be silly. Just call me Lizzy."

Lizzy then wraps her arm around my shoulder and gives a squeeze. "Come in, girls, come in!"

We follow her into the house, and I can't help but gasp at how beautiful and grandiose everything is. It is unlike anything I have ever seen before.

"I can't believe you live here," I say breathlessly. "It's like a castle."

Lizzy laughs. "I'm just so glad you girls agreed to do the interview with me," she says.

Jana stops abruptly in front of me. "Interview?"

"Surprise!" my dad laughs. "Since you two wanted to play detectives, you get to share your amazing knowledge on camera."

"No, dad, please don't make me go on camera," Jana pleads.

"Jana, it's not going to be that bad. I think it's kind of neat," I say.

Jana just looks at me as if I have five eyeballs. Her face looks pale, and for a second, I think she might even throw up. I had forgotten all about Jana's horrible stage fright until now. During her 6th grade concert, she ran off stage crying.

"Dad, since I forced Jana to let me solve the case, do you think I can just do the interview alone?"

My dad thinks it over, "I guess so, though I thought this was going to be a punishment for you too," he laughs.

"Don't you have stage fright too?"

"Me? Of course not! I'm a natural."

"What about that time in second grade when you passed out in front of everyone at the spelling bee?" Jana reminds me.

"That was ages ago," I laugh. "Plus, I'm not actually spelling words in front of people right now. I'm just talking into a camera."

"Blondie, can you come sit next to me?" Lizzy asks sweetly from her oversized living room.

I take a seat next to her and look at the giant camera that is inches from my face.

"That seems really close up," I say.

"It just looks that way," a cameraman says. "Don't worry, it will look completely normal when everyone watches the news."

I swallow hard. *Don't think about all the people watching. Just pretend you're talking to Lizzy.*

"Are you ready, Lizzy, darling?" an older woman's voice calls from the other room.

"All ready, Bev," Lizzy replies.

A short woman in a skirt suit walks in, and I recognize her immediately from the local news channel. She sits down in a chair next to us and smiles at the camera.

"Welcome back to Channel 5 news. Not all us get the chance to say that we have met our favorite celebrity, but this past weekend, one fan not only met her favorite popstar but also saved her life.

I'm Beverly Truman, and today, I am in the house of superstar, Lizzy Lizard, and her super fan, Blondelle McGhee."

I feel myself blush as the woman calls me by my full name. Only my parents call me "Blondelle" when they are mad at me. It's not that I hate the name, it's just a little weird. I was named after a great-great French grandmother or something like that.

"Lizzy, what happened when you went on stage that night?" Bev asks with a dramatic dose of concern in her voice.

"It was horrible, Bev. One moment I am ready to sing my heart out, and the next thing I know, my head is throbbing, and I am being raced to the hospital." Lizzy wipes at an imaginary tear to make her story seem sadder.

Bev shook her head out of disbelief. "To think you came so close to dying. How does that make you feel?"

"It was scary. I am just so thankful that Blondie was there."

Bev focuses her attention on me. "Blondelle, or do you prefer Blondie? How does it feel to save a celebrity's life?"

"I...um..." I struggle getting the right words out. "You can call me Blondie, and I didn't save her life. I just helped figure out what happened that night."

"Incredible. Tell me, how can such a young girl uncover such a big case?"

"Well, it was actually my sister, Jana…" I pause when I see Jana waving her hands at me on the other side of the room. She shakes her head furiously and mouths "No" several times. "I mean, we just followed the clues and asked a lot of questions. I had a feeling that Lizzy falling wasn't an accident."

"And how do you feel, Lizzy, knowing your own agent's daughter tried to kill you?" Bev asks, turning her attention back to Lizzy.

"She wasn't trying to kill her," I interrupt. Bev smiles politely at me, but I can tell by the way she looks at me she doesn't want me to talk anymore.

"My apologies," Bev begins again, making sure I won't say another word. "Lizzy, how does it feel to be betrayed by your own agent's daughter?"

I tune out the rest of the interview. Lizzy got so much of the story wrong, but Bev wasn't interested in hearing my side. She would just find a way to redirect the question back to Lizzy.

CHAPTER ELEVEN

I'd Rather Be a Detective

"You did great, champ," my dad says once we get back in the car.

"Thanks, dad," I sigh, putting my chin on my hand. I stare out the window.

"What's wrong?" my dad asks.

"Lizzy exaggerated so much of the story and made everything sound worse than it was."

My dad lets out a laugh. "Welcome to show business, honey. Interviewers like Bev only want to hear the juicy part of the story, even if the story isn't entirely true."

"But Lizzy wasn't helping either," I say. "She wasn't even there when Jana and I solved the case."

My dad looks over at me sympathetically and smiles.

"Lizzy is still a good person, but sometimes celebrities get caught up in doing silly things to get attention."

"I just thought she was different," I sigh again.

"Did I ever tell you about the time I met my favorite celebrity?" my dad asks.

"You have a favorite celebrity?" Jana asks.

My dad chuckles. "Yes, of course. Don't you remember that one TV show I watched all the time?"

"*Kung Fu Spy*," Jana and I shout out together and burst into laughter.

"Yes, that one. Well, I never told anyone, but the actor of that movie came to the Epic Center to arrange an event. I was so excited to meet him, but all he did was yell at the Epic Center employees and complain. It was a big bummer."

"Is that why you don't watch *Kung Fu Spy* anymore?" Jana asks.

"That's exactly why. The show is just not the same for me after I met him. Celebrities are just people, like me and you, and sometimes they are not as magical in real life as they are on the TV screen or in your case, in their songs."

"I think I will still listen to her music, but I'm definitely never going to do another interview with her." The whole car breaks into laughter.

"Besides," Jana adds. "Being a detective is so much cooler than being a rock star."

"Does this mean you want to help me solve more cases?" I ask.

"I wouldn't go that far," Jana says with a big smile. "I'll leave the mysteries to you."

Made in the USA
Middletown, DE
20 September 2017